ONCE UPON A TIMELESS TALE

The Three Billy Goats Gruff

STORY BY **ASBJØRNSEN** & **MOE**
RETOLD BY **MARGRETE LAMOND**

PICTURES BY
GAYE CHAPMAN

LITTLE HARE
www.littleharebooks.com

Once upon a time—in the bad old days, when trolls were trolls— there lived three smelly goats. Their names—all three—were Billy Goat Gruff.

They were not just smelly, but bony and thin, so they headed for the mountain meadows where the grass grew sweet and green, and where they could make themselves fat.

On the way up the path was a bridge for crossing a waterfall, and under the bridge lived a troll.

The troll was as big as a boulder, and twice as ugly too, with eyes like tin trays, and a nose longer than a rake handle.

But off they went, anyway, those billy goats, and first to cross the bridge was the youngest Billy Goat Gruff.

Tripp trapp, tripp trapp, went the billy goat, so that the bridge trembled and swayed.

'Who's that tripping over my bridge,' shrieked the troll from underneath, 'making it tremble and sway?'

The troll gnashed its teeth so hard that sparks flew off them.

'It is the littlest Billy Goat Gruff,' squeaked the youngest goat. 'I'm on my way to the meadows to make myself fat.'

'No, you're not,' roared the troll, 'because I'm coming out to gobble you up!'

'Oh no, don't eat me, I'm as bony as can be,' cried the goat, brave as he could manage, which wasn't very brave at all.

'My brother will be along any minute, and he is much bigger than I am.'

'Go on, then,' growled the troll. 'I might as well wait for two mouthfuls later instead of having one now.'

And before the troll could so much as roll its eyes, the littlest Billy Goat Gruff had scampered across the bridge and run away up the mountain.

The troll didn't have to wait long before the middle Billy Goat Gruff arrived.

Trippety trappety, trippety trappety, went his hooves, so that the bridge shuddered and shook.

'Who's that trippety-trapping over my bridge?' shrieked the troll, as if it didn't know. 'Who's that making it shudder and shake?'

And it clenched its fists so hard its knuckles popped.

'It is the middle Billy Goat Gruff,' said the goat. 'I'm on my way to the meadows to make myself fat.'

'Oh no, you're not,' roared the troll, 'because I'm going to gobble you up!'

'Don't bother with me, I'm as thin as can be,' sang the goat, who was much braver than the other one. 'If you will only wait a bit, my brother will be along, and he is much, much bigger than I am.'

The troll wasn't very clever. 'Go on, then,' it growled. 'I might as well wait for four mouthfuls later instead of having two now.'

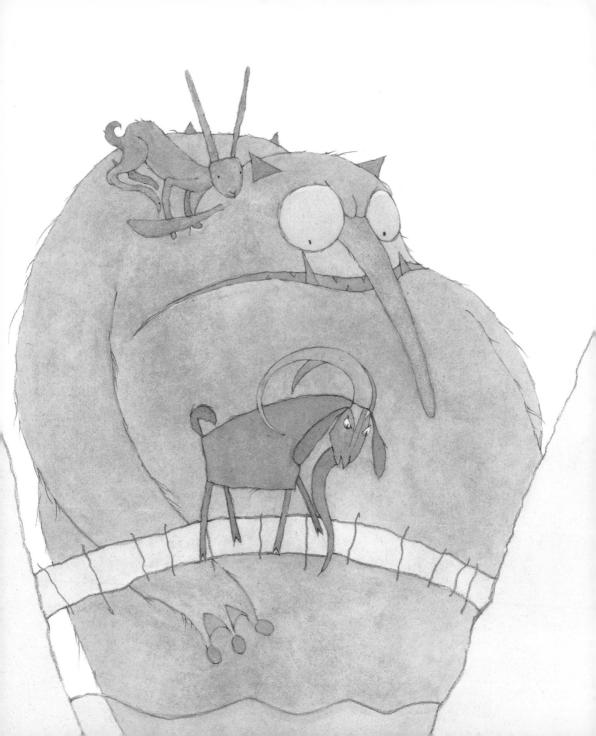

And before the troll could so much as shrug its shoulders, the middle Billy Goat Gruff had galloped across the bridge and run away up to the mountain meadows.

There was barely time for the troll to blink before the biggest Billy Goat Gruff came along.

Tripp trapp, tripp trapp, tripp trapp, went his hooves—this goat was so big and strong and heavy that the timbers groaned and shuddered.

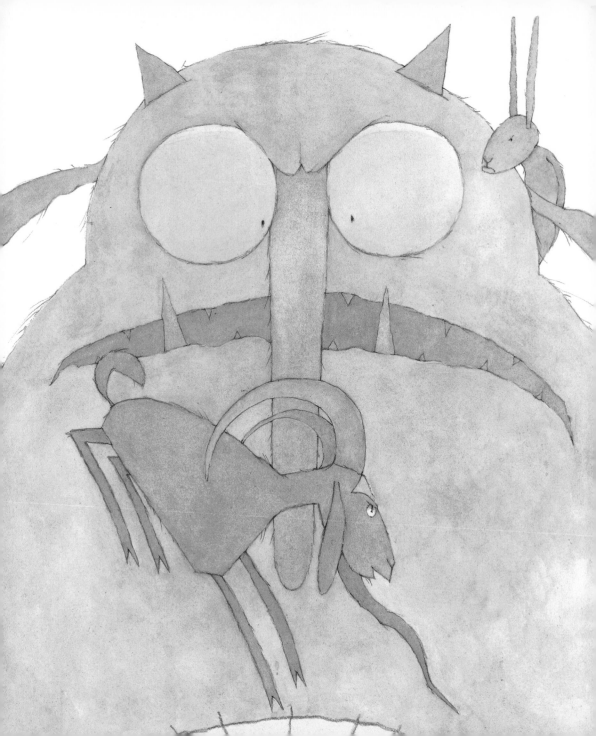

'Who's that stamping on my bridge,' shrieked the troll, although it must have guessed by now, 'making it shudder and quake?'

And it ground its teeth and clenched its fists so hard that it ran with sweat.

'It is the biggest Billy Goat Gruff,' growled the goat. 'I'm heading up the mountain to make myself nice and fat.'

'Oh no, you're not,' roared the troll. 'I'm coming out and I'm going to gobble you up!'

'Out you come!' cried the goat, bold as brass and brave as anything. 'Because then I'll use my horns like spears and poke your eyeballs out your ears!'

That's what he said, and it's exactly what he did. He charged at the troll and poked out its eyes with his horns.

Then, because the troll was a troll and deserved no better, the biggest Billy Goat Gruff stamped on the troll's bones until they broke to pieces, and tossed it out over the waterfall.

When that was done, the biggest Billy Goat Gruff headed away up the mountain to where his brothers were waiting, and where the grass was sweet and green.

—

And there those billy goats stayed.

And there they grew fat—so fat that they almost couldn't drag themselves home at the end of summer.

And if they're still not fat—well, they must have grown thin again. Which means *snip snap snout*, the tale is told out.

Little Hare Books
an imprint of
Hardie Grant Egmont
Ground Floor, Building 1, 658 Church Street
Richmond, Victoria 3121, Australia

www.littleharebooks.com

Cataloguing-in-Publication details are available from the
National Library of Australia

978 1 742974 00 2 (hbk.)

Designed by Vida & Luke Kelly
Produced by Pica Digital, Singapore
Printed in China by Wai Man Book Binding Ltd.

5 4 3 2 1